The Horse Across the Quaggy

Written by Chris Powling

Illustrated by Martin Ursell

Collins

1. HOLIDAY JOB

Every morning when he got up, Archie pulled back his bedroom curtains, pressed his nose against the windowpane and stared at the Big House across the river. "Still there, then?" he'd say.

Then he'd laugh at himself. After all, a building doesn't disappear overnight. Especially a building like the Big House. The real surprise for Archie was why the Big House was there at all. "I mean, just look at it!" he grinned at Spud and Lola on the first day of the school holidays. "Everything about the place is *wrong*!"

"Is it?" said Spud.

"Looks sort of grand to me," said Lola.

"Grand, maybe," Archie sniffed, "if you miss all the cracks in the stonework and the windows they've boarded up. Besides, why is it on the far side of the Quaggy? It's this side of the river, on the Quaggy Estate, where people actually live. Look what's over there! How come it's stuck between a superstore and some sort of timber yard?"

"Yes, but they came much later," Lola said. "I bet the Big House got there first."

"In the olden days," said Spud.

"Exactly," Lola nodded. "There was probably once a whole row of houses, just like the Big House. Eventually they got knocked down to make way for the new stuff."

"So why not the Big House as well?" Archie asked. "Why was it left there all on its own?"

This was a good question. Archie's window was wide open now to catch whatever breeze there was on the drowsy summer afternoon. Lola and Spud watched a gigantic lorry pull into the service bay behind the superstore.

3

They heard the buzz of heavy-duty saws in the
timber yard and the low rumble of traffic from the slip
road on to the motorway. The Big House stayed still
and silent.

There seemed to be a gap of at least a hundred years
between it and each of its neighbours. Yes, its walls
were webbed with cracks. Yes, some of its windows
were boarded up. Even so, it was easy enough to
imagine a coach with six white horses pulling up at
the huge oak doors that fronted the lawn, which ran
down to the Quaggy.

Spud frowned, thoughtfully. "I wonder who lives there," he said.

"That's if anyone lives there," said Lola.

"Oh, somebody does," said Archie. He tucked his hands behind his head and sank back against the cushions on his bed. There was a faint smile on his lips.

"You know who lives there, don't you?" said Lola, suspiciously.

"Do I?"

"You're setting us up," said Spud.

"Think so?"

"Archie, I'm not in the mood for one of your games."

"It's not a game, Spud. It may not even be fun – it may be dead boring as well as hard work."

"What will?" asked Lola.

"Tell us," Spud growled.

Archie's smile broadened. "It's my mum," he said. "She does this cleaning work, you see ... and last week she got a new job, Mondays and Tuesdays. The customer's a bit posh, Mum says, but really sweet. She hopes it'll be a nice little earner."

"So where do we come in?"

"Ah ..." said Archie. "I'm glad you asked me that, Spud."

He sat up and swung his feet back on the bedroom floor.
He seemed to be weighing his words as he spoke. "This
new lady of Mum's has got a job she needs doing," he
told them. "It'll only take two or three days, she says.
She needs some kids she can trust to tidy her attic – right
now it looks like a pigsty. She wants the good stuff sorted
from the bad, mainly, so that it looks more like a storeroom
and less like a rubbish tip. She'll pay the same hourly rate
that Mum gets. Mum's a bit miffed about that!"

"Three kids like us?" said Lola, shocked.

"The same hourly rate your mum gets?" Spud said in disbelief.

"That's if you're willing to take it on," Archie shrugged. "If you are, we won't have far to go. You see, Mum's new client lives on the other side of the Quaggy – at the Big House."

Spud and Lola didn't speak. They didn't need to. All three of them were back at the window now, gazing across the river at a building that had no business being there. Not in a world of superstores and timber yards. The Big House shimmered like a mirage in the heavy July heat. It looked more than ever like a leftover from the olden days.

2. COPIES

It was Archie's mum who introduced them. "Here they are," she said. "Three youngsters who won't let you down!"

"I'm sure they won't," said Lady Hartnip.

"I've already explained what they've got to do. And they're really keen to get started. Isn't that right, kids?"

"Yes, I am," said Spud.

"Me too," said Lola.

"And me," said Archie.

His mother beamed. "Shall I leave them with you? So you can get to know them before you decide if they're up to the job?"

"That's so kind, Mrs Satchwell. You're a real treasure. Shall I see you again next Monday at 9 o'clock?"

"Monday it is ... on the dot."

As Archie's Mum turned away, she gave all three of them a sharp, don't-let-me-down sort of look. The tall oak doors left a faint echo hanging in the air as they banged behind her.

Lady Hartnip paused for a moment. For someone as old and posh as she was, she seemed strangely shy. She blinked uncertainly over her half-moon spectacles and leant a little harder on her black, silver-topped walking stick. "You look like the perfect team to me," she said. "The job may be far from perfect for you, though. It'll take three days at most, I'd say, counting today. May I show you round the house before we go up to the attic? Then you can decide for yourselves if you want to go ahead."

Lady Hartnip's visitors looked at each other in surprise. Was she interviewing them or were they interviewing her?

For once, Archie was on his best behaviour. "Sounds like a good idea to me," he said. "That OK with you two?"

"Fine," said Lola.

"Lead on," said Spud.

Lady Hartnip's eyes twinkled. Could she be pulling their legs? No, surely not. Posh old ladies in half-moon spectacles, who carry a silver-topped stick, don't go in for teasing, do they? Or do they?

She lifted the stick and pointed. "We can start here in the hall if you like."

"The hall?" asked Spud. "I thought this was the sitting-room."

"Designed to impress," said Lady Hartnip, wistfully. "And that's what it did, of course, once upon a time."

They could see that. The carpets, which weren't even wall-to-wall, would have covered the floor in their own houses five times over. The furniture reminded them of the stuff you saw on that travelling antiques show on TV. As for the paintings, almost all of them looked ... well, famous.

Lola peered at them curiously. "Hey," she said, "it looks like a museum in here."

"Or an art gallery," Lady Hartnip laughed. "The landscape over the fireplace is by an artist called Gainsborough. The portrait next to it is a Van Dyck and the horse picture by the door was painted by Sir George Stubbs. They were very famous in their day."

"Are the paintings precious, then?"

"They'd be worth a pretty penny, Lola ... if they were genuine. Unfortunately, all three are copies. My family had to sell the originals many years ago. First, most of the land had to go, then the furniture and the pictures. This house just eats up money, I'm afraid. Are the three of you keen on famous art?"

"Not really," said Lola, "but I go to this painting club after school. It's run by Mr Danziger, who's really cool. He says we can't hope to be proper artists 'til we've seen what the best-ever painters have already done. Every week he shows us a picture just like the ones you've got here. He makes us study it for ages."

"He sounds like an excellent teacher. What about you two lads? Do you belong to this wonderful club?"

"Nah," said Archie. "I've got football training after school."

"And I've got IT," Spud said. "I wouldn't mind joining Mr Danziger's club one day, though. Now I've had a look at the real thing, I mean."

"Not quite the real thing, I'm afraid."

15

The old lady turned away. As she led them up through the house, she showed them other carpets and other furniture and other paintings, which also weren't quite the real thing. Finally, after the third floor, most of the walls were bare, but showing lighter patches from time to time where a map or a picture had once been hung. "Eventually, we couldn't even afford the copies," she explained. "All the money we raised had to go on the roof, or the brickwork, or the foundations."

"Or the garden," whispered Archie, a little too loudly. "That looks pretty tatty as well – all the yellow grass and scraggy hedges."

Suddenly, he saw the sharp looks he was getting from
Spud and Lola. "What's wrong with you two?" he hissed,
indignantly. "I'm only telling the truth."

Spud and Lola rolled their eyes.

Not that Lady Hartnip noticed. Was she deaf or just in
a dream? Her silver-topped cane went on tap-tap-tapping
upstairs until they reached the last landing of all. In front
of them now was a narrow set of steps that led to a broad,
large, square trapdoor overhead.

She stared up at it and smiled. "We've arrived at last," she said. "This is one of the entrances into the attic."

"One of them?" asked Spud.

"There are four altogether, I think. Or is it five? It's quite a large attic, you see. It stretches right across the house."

"And you want all of it sorted out?" Archie frowned. "With just the three of us to do it?"

"Well, I was hoping ..."

"It'll be fine," Lola cut in. "More than three and we'd be tripping over each other. Sometimes a team can be too big, OK? Have you got that, Spud? Got that, Archie?"

Archie's grumble died on his lips. Lola had taken to Lady Hartnip, he could tell. And you didn't argue with Lola in that sort of mood. Besides, how often do you get the chance to explore the attic in a crumbling old mansion like this one? What sort of things might they find? Just thinking about it sent a tingle of excitement down his spine.

19

3. IN THE ATTIC

Archie's excitement didn't last long. That first day was the worst. By the second day they'd almost got used to the handkerchiefs they tied over their faces to stop them choking in the dust. They'd almost got used to the size of the attic, too – or should that be attics, since it was split into lots of separate spaces? These were lit by tiny dormer windows where dust-motes floated in shafts of sunlight made dim and dingy by the quaint, old-fashioned glass.

What they didn't get used to was the heat. It gummed up their hair. It stuck their clothes to their backs. It blinded them with the sweat that ran into their eyes.

Lola wrinkled her nose as she refolded a moth-eaten rug that was caked with dust. "This is dirty work," she said.

"And dead boring," said Spud.

"Tomorrow it'll be over," Archie pointed out. "And Elizabeth will have got what Mum calls a 'good job jobbed'."

That's what they called her now – Elizabeth. Not Lady Hartnip, or Your Ladyship, or Ma'am.

"I can't bear it," she'd said. "It makes me feel so old and stuffy. Though Hugo won't like me saying that."

"Who's Hugo?"

"He's my nephew, Spud. Hugo's all the family I have now. Not that we always see eye-to-eye. It was Hugo who left the attic in such a mess after searching for ... well, for anything of value, really. Anything to help us to keep the house going. One day, after I'm gone, it'll fall entirely on Hugo's shoulders. Sometimes I even wonder myself if it's fair to burden him with the Big House."

"Can't you sell the place?" Archie had asked.

"Never," said Elizabeth.

"Why not?"

"This house was built for our family more than 400 years ago. We've lived here ever since – Hartnip after Hartnip after Hartnip. It's part of our history, part of who we are. How could I possibly turn my back on everything that makes me a Hartnip? Giving up is not an option."

Her face had tightened like a mask. She sighed and left the room, looking so small and thin that a puff of wind could blow her away. They hadn't seen her since.

"She was really worried," said Lola, remembering this.

"Worried?"

"About the future, Spud. She wants Hartnips to live in this house forever. She's not stupid, though. Deep down, she knows that may not happen. She's not even sure this nephew of hers is on her side."

"Lola, we've not even met him!" Archie exclaimed.

"See if I'm not right," said Lola, darkly. She stared across the river. Bent crooked by the window's ancient glass, the houses across the Quaggy seemed to be melting like a set of waxworks under the blaze of the July sky.

Most of the time they were too busy to talk. They piled all the useless stuff by the window for Elizabeth – or maybe her nephew – to inspect at the end of the day. All the good stuff they left in neat, orderly piles wherever they found it. They opened tea chests. They cleared shelves. They turned boxes upside-down and inside-out. They reached into nooks and crannies and corners. They began to wonder how even a house as old as this one could have gathered quite so many cast-offs.

At midday they stopped to eat the sandwiches Elizabeth had made them.

"That's the trouble with a job like this," said Archie, munching hard, "most of the time it's really dull, yet it still fills your head. You can't even daydream while you're doing it."

"Daydream about what?" Spud asked.

"Disneyland," said Archie at once. "That's the holiday Mum always promises me when she's saved up enough."

Spud smiled, wryly. "We'll be off to Granny's as usual. It's fine ... but it's not exactly Disneyland."

"Neither is our caravan by the sea," said Lola. "Disneyland would be really great. I wouldn't care which one – I'd settle for any one of them."

"So would I," Archie sighed. "Disneyland's like another world compared with this junk yard in the sky."

"At least we're not stuck here all our lives, Archie."

"What's that supposed to mean?"

15

Lola folded her hanky and mopped her brow.
"I'm thinking of Elizabeth," she said. "OK, so she loves this house to bits. But if you ask me it's more of a trap than a home."

All three of them went quiet. It was as if the tap-tap-tap of a silver-topped cane was echoing like a heartbeat through this house of fake carpets, fake paintings and fake furniture. What startled them back to reality was the sudden creak of the trapdoor behind them – followed by the clatter of heavy footsteps.

"I'm looking for Auntie's little helpers!" came a crisp, commanding voice. "Is everything spick and span yet?"

Elizabeth's nephew Hugo had arrived.

4. HUGO

Hugo was younger than they'd expected. His hair was long and floppy, he wore a cream-coloured summer suit and his eyes were the coldest they'd ever seen. "You must be Archie," he said.

"That's me."

"And you're Spud."

"You've got it."

"So you over there must be Lola."

"Well spotted," Lola grinned.

"My name is Hugo Hartnip-Hollister. As you probably know, I'm the owner of this place."

"Really?" said Archie in surprise. "That's news to us. We thought it belonged to Lady Hartnip downstairs."

Hugo's cold eyes narrowed. Casually, he pushed back his quiff of hair. "Excuse that slip of the tongue," he said, smoothly. "You're absolutely right, of course. Aunt Elizabeth is the current owner. I can't actually say this wreck of a house is mine until ..." He broke off.

27

It was Lola who came to his rescue, "Until you're the next Hartnip in charge?" she said, tactfully.

"Don't be sad about it," said Archie, trying to help. "My Mum says dainty little old ladies like Elizabeth can go on forever. She'll probably outlive you!"

"That wouldn't surprise me," replied her nephew.

He glanced around the attic as if he'd welcome a change of subject. With the toe of his highly polished shoe, he turned over one or two items piled under the window. "This is the rubbish heap?" he asked.

"So far," said Lola.

"There's bound to be more, though," Spud said. "We're only chucking out the broken stuff. Or the stuff that's so battered and bent you wouldn't even take it to a boot sale."

"Have you put anything aside for yourselves?"

"What?"

"Everything's still here, is it?"

Spud's face was stony. On either side of him, Archie and Lola stiffened.

"Touched a nerve, have I?" sneered the man in the suit. As he lounged against the window, almost blotting out the sunlight, his shadow spilled across the attic floor. Even on a day as muggy as this it looked like a patch of black ice. Everything about him told them he was the kind of grown-up who couldn't stand children ... or most other grown-ups, come to that. "Let me make myself clear," Hugo continued. "My aunt is too easy-going by half. Almost anyone can take advantage of her.

But I'm not so sentimental. I'll be watching the three of you closely. If there's any mischief while you're here, you'll be answering to me."

"Like nicking stuff, you mean?"

"Who knows, Archie? Or a bit of vandalism, maybe? Isn't that how you kids get your kicks nowadays?"

Archie lifted an eyebrow. "Well, if it is, we're out of luck. There's nothing here worth nicking. As for vandalising the place, just look at the bits we haven't tidied yet. How could you tell if we did?"

Hugo blinked. "Two very good points," he said. "Maybe I've been a little hard on you. I only wish Aunt Elizabeth saw things as clearly. All she cares about is preserving the family heritage – which seems to begin and end with this house."

"You don't agree?" Lola asked.

"Times change, young lady. And a sensible person – Hartnip or otherwise – changes with them. Nowadays, only a banker, a pop star, or some sort of business tycoon can afford a house like this. And people of that sort don't want to be stuck between a superstore and a timber yard."

"And the Quaggy Estate opposite," Archie added.

"That, too."

"So what's your plan?" asked Lola, quickly.

"My plan?"

"For the house," she nodded. "I mean, it's falling to bits. Anybody can see that. So something's got to be done."

Elizabeth's nephew eyed her warily. Had he said too much? He sighed and flicked a speck of dust off his jacket.

"That's my concern," he said. "Your concern is to do whatever her ladyship has instructed – nothing more and nothing less. Remember, these days she reports everything back to me. I like to keep track of what's going on."

"Fair enough," said Archie.

"Don't let us keep you," said Spud.

Lola smiled her politest smile. "It's time we got back on the job, anyway," she said.

A faint frown creased Hugo's face. It was almost as if they were dismissing him, rather than the other way round. He glanced back at them as he lowered the trapdoor behind him. All he saw was a pile of assorted oddments lit by a shaft of murky sunlight. Archie, Lola and Spud had already vanished into another part of the attic.

5. THE SACK IN THE CUPBOARD

"What a charmer!" Archie exclaimed.

"A tough guy, though," said Spud. He flicked an imaginary speck of dust off his T-shirt. "That's my concern," he said in an exact copy of Hugo's voice. "Your concern is to do whatever her ladyship has instructed!"

"Except she isn't like that at all," said Archie. "She doesn't instruct you to do anything. She sort of asks it as a favour."

"She's a lovely lady," said Spud.

"Pity she's got such a creep for a nephew."

"Not a total creep, Archie," said Lola. "For one thing, I bet he's dead right about this house."

The boys stared at her in surprise. She was crouching on her hands and knees, half-in and half-out of a low cupboard tucked under the eaves.

"I thought you were on Elizabeth's side?" Archie said. "Hugo will dump this place like a shot as soon as he gets his hands on it."

"So would anyone who's got half a brain. You can't just ignore the condition it's in. It must cost a fortune simply to keep it standing up. Hugo may be a bit of a pain compared with Elizabeth, but that doesn't mean he's not right. At least he can see the house is doomed. You said it yourself, Archie – everything about the place is wrong. The trouble is, Elizabeth would rather die than admit it."

"Yes, but ..."

"That doesn't mean ..."

The boys were floundering and they knew it. Luckily for them, Lola had already ducked back in the cupboard.

"Looks empty to me," said Spud, peering round her. "Are you sure there's anything in there?"

"Some sort of sack," Lola said.

"A sack?"

"It's got caught on a nail, I think. I'm trying to work it loose. There, that's done it!"

"It's a sack all right," said Archie. "What's inside?"

Lola sat back with her legs tucked under her, the sack solid and heavy on her lap. She picked at the knot that fastened one end of it. It was an old, flat knot that resisted even her nimble fingers. She gritted her teeth. "Can't seem to get this thing undone ..."

Then, suddenly, the sack was open.

A vase slipped out of its covering, bumped over Lola's knees and rolled across the attic floor. It would have gone on rolling as far as the trapdoor if Spud hadn't put out a hand to stop it. Carefully, he stood it the right way up where the sunbeam from the dormer window caught it like a spotlight. "Well, look at that!" he exclaimed.

Archie and Lola were already looking. It was hard not to. Whether you liked the vase, or whether you didn't, its shape and design and colouring would have caught anyone's eye.

Archie scratched his head. "It's got a kind of ... Chinese feel to it," he said.

"Old, though," said Spud.

"As old as this house, maybe," Archie agreed. "Except it's in perfect condition. What do you think, Lola?"

"Not sure."

But something was bothering her.
They could tell from her puzzled
frown and the way she was biting
her lip. Also, she was tugging at
an earlobe. This was a sure sign she had
something on her mind.

"Come on, Lola," Archie prompted.
"Spit it out!"

Lola shook her head. "It's daft,"
she said.

"Who cares?" said Spud.

"OK, but no teasing? You see, last term at Art Club,
Mr Danziger showed us a newspaper cutting. It was a
report about a Chinese vase that had just fetched a world
record price at auction. That's why it was in the news.
And this one looks just like it."

"You're pulling our legs," Archie grinned.

"I'm not," said Lola. "Truly I'm not."

"So what was the price?"

"Promise you won't laugh?"

"Promise," Spud said.

"Me too," said Archie.

When Lola spoke, though, she was laughing softly to herself. "Look," she said, "I'm talking about months ago. The picture they printed of the vase has gone all blurry in my mind. All I can remember for sure is what the vase cost."

Archie gave a snort of impatience. "Lola, stop dithering," he growled. "Just tell us how much it was!"

"£50 million," Lola said.

6. SEARCHING THE INTERNET

The library stayed open late that day, so there was no need to leave work early. Not that Elizabeth would have objected if they had.

"The attic has never looked tidier, my dears!" she'd said. "It's such a weight off my mind knowing I'll be leaving everything to Hugo in such good order. Will you really finish tomorrow, do you think?"

"Probably," said Archie. "That's if we don't get heatstroke. It's like a furnace up there under the roof."

"Oh dear ..."

"Take no notice of him, Elizabeth," Spud interrupted. "Archie loves having a good moan."

"Well, if you really think ..."

"Everything's fine, honestly. No worries at all. We'll see you in the morning, shall we?"

"I'll be here as usual, my dears." She waved to them from the bottom of her garden until they got as far as the road bridge.

41

Here they turned left over the Quaggy. Or what was left of the Quaggy. There was more mud than water now. Not to mention more rubbish. Most of the year this lay hidden under the slow, green, greasy water, but not in the drought of mid-summer.

"Reckon that should be our next job," said Spud. "Once we've got the attic sorted we'll start on the river. We'll be looking for something to do."

"Good idea," Archie sniggered. "Who knows, we might find another vase worth £50 million."

"Very funny," said Lola.

It had been Spud's idea to call at the library on their way home. "We can check it out on the internet," he'd said. "Just to make sure you've got the details right, Lola ... all 50 million of them."

"Thanks," said Lola, sarcastically.

From the outside, their local library looked almost as old and scruffy as the Big House. But inside it was bright and buzzing – even now in the summer holidays.

"Over to you, Spud," Archie said. "You can take the lead here. This is your area."

"Yeah," Spud grinned, "my area."

They soon found a vacant workstation. Carefully, Spud angled the computer screen away from the main room. "You never know who's looking over your shoulder," he winked.

"Like Hugo Hartnip-Hollister?"

"Especially him, Archie."

Spud looked up from the keyboard. "OK," he said. "Let's get searching. What shall I put in the box?"

"How about 'Vase worth £50 million'?"

"Sounds good to me!"

"You just wait," said Lola, gritting her teeth.

They didn't have to wait long. The instant Spud tapped in the words "Vase worth ..." the screen sprang to life. According to the internet, there were more than four million hits ahead of them. One of the entries had a headline that said it all.

**CLEANING LADY
FINDS VASE WORTH
£50 MILLION**

"Just like us ..." Archie whispered.

"Told you," said Lola.

Spud scrolled them through the story three times before they felt they'd properly got to grips with it:

> How would you like to find a Chinese vase worth £50 million on your first day at work? This is exactly what happened last autumn to a cleaning lady who was tidying the basement of an ordinary London house. Yesterday the vase was sold at auction for £50 million.
>
> Experts say the vase probably left China about 150 years ago and was sold on to a private purchaser about a century later. After that, its history is anyone's guess ...

Even better than the report itself was the full-colour picture that filled the screen. To say they stared at every detail of the vase would be an understatement. What they actually did was gawp.

Outside, on the front steps of the library, they checked their print-out yet again.

"Identical," Archie declared. "The two vases are identical. Just think, our vase might be worth £50 million!"

"Archie, it doesn't work like that with antiques," said Spud. "With them, what really counts is how rare they are."

"So two vases being half as rare as one vase ..."

"... makes them only half as valuable. Which means the vase we've got here is worth £25 million at most. Unless more of them turn up, of course. In that case, the price will nosedive."

"Wow!" said Archie.

Behind them, reflected in the glass doors of the library, the three attic cleaners gazed at each other in alarm.

"We'd better hand this vase over as soon as we can," said Spud, with a nervous laugh. "Before so many of them crop up that they start selling at two-a-penny!"

"Who do we hand it to, though?" Lola asked.

"Elizabeth, of course."

"And what's the first thing she'll do?"

"Tell Hugo, I suppose."

"Exactly," Lola said. "And where do you think that'll get her? Will he really let her restore the Big House to its former glory – with a superstore to the right and a timber yard to the left? He'll see it as wasting millions of pounds on a project that's completely pointless."

"That's how you see it, don't you?"

"Yes, I do, Archie," said Lola, miserably. "But I'm not Elizabeth. Honestly, you'd think a stack of money like this – that's if there is a stack of money – would solve everybody's problems. Instead, it may do the opposite. It could force their differences out into the open!"

"Right," said Archie.

"It might," Spud agreed.

Suddenly, the vase they'd left behind at the Big House felt more like trouble than treasure.

7. THE HARDEST THING IN THE WORLD

They should have guessed she'd notice. That evening,
as soon as Archie's mum got home, she spotted
their mood.

"Hi kids!" she said. "How was the job today?"

"Fine," said Spud.

"Really good," Lola said.

"And you'll be finished tomorrow as expected?"

"Should do," Spud nodded.

"So what's the problem?" asked Mrs Satchwell.

"Problem?" said Archie. "What problem?"

"The problem that's got all three of you looking so glum;
that problem. I'm not dim, you know."

After that, it all came flooding out. It would have been
simpler if they'd taken turns, but they were far too wound
up for that. Their voices tumbled over each other, and
cut each other up, until eventually Mrs Satchwell clapped
her hands. "Hey," she said, "one at a time, OK?"

Lola did most of the talking. Spud and Archie just added a
few details here and there. Mrs Satchwell sat at the kitchen
table, with Spud's print-out in front of her and her eyes
growing wider and wider. "Well!" she said when they'd
finished. "What a story!"

"Yeah, it's a story all right," said Spud, ruefully. "What we want to know is ... how's it going to end?"

"I've no idea," said Archie's mum. "Happily, I hope. After all, you've handled things pretty well so far."

"Have we?" asked Archie.

"Better than most kids, I'd say. If the vase in the attic and the vase on the internet really are the same, that's enough to give anyone goosebumps – me included. Spud's right to be wary, though. Only an expert can decide what it's really worth."

"But it must have some value," Lola wailed, "and whatever that turns out to be, it'll spark off a row between Elizabeth and Hugo. They just don't agree about the Big House."

"I've already seen that for myself, Lola. They're as different as chalk and cheese, that pair."

"So what do we do about it, Mum?" asked Archie.

"Nothing, son."

"What?"

Archie's mum sat back in her chair. She folded the photocopy neatly in half and pushed it across the table to Spud. For a moment, she looked down at her work-worn hands as if to check she'd got a proper grip on what they'd told her. "There's nothing you can do," she said at last. "It's up to Elizabeth and Hugo. It's their house, their vase and their decision, OK? Nobody can make it for them."

"But Mrs Satchwell ..."

"Lola, they must sort it out for themselves."

"I know that, but ..." Lola's voice trailed away. She gave Archie and Spud a nudge for back-up, but they were lost for words as well.

"Exactly," said Mrs Satchwell. "Tomorrow you must finish the job in the attic, team. Then you must give the vase to its rightful owners, the Hartnips, and walk away without looking back. That won't be easy, of course, I realise that. Sometimes doing nothing is the hardest thing in the world."

8. JOB DONE

It was teatime before they'd finished. By then, the entire attic was immaculate. "Looks like a soldier's kit laid out for inspection," Archie said. "All squared-off and squeaky clean."

"When were you in the army?" Spud scoffed.

"I might be one day."

"Oh ... right."

"Got the vase?" asked Lola.

"Here," said Archie, "still in its sack."

They shut the trapdoor carefully behind them. At the top of the main staircase, they paused a moment by the huge window. The slip road on to the motorway looked closer than ever. Darker, too. A rim of cloud was advancing from the horizon like a lid dragged across the boiling blue sky.

"Storm coming," Spud said.

"Good," said Archie. "It'll cool things down."

Elizabeth and her nephew were on the terrace in front of the house, sipping tea from small, white cups. "Would you care for some refreshment, my dears?" she asked.

"Perhaps they don't take tea," said Hugo.

"No, we don't," Archie said, "not really. But thanks, anyway. We've come to tell you that we've finished all the tidying upstairs. Oh, and to show you something –"

"That you've left the attic in tip-top condition?" enquired Hugo.

"I'd say it's pretty much perfect," replied Archie.

"It had better be, Archie. I could hardly believe my ears when I heard what you're charging for the job," grumbled Hugo.

"Hugo, dear ..." intervened Elizabeth. She lowered
her teacup on to the spindly table beside her. Her smile
was as sweet as ever, but her voice had a sharpness they
hadn't picked up before. "I suggested the payment myself,"
she said. "And from what I've seen of their efforts, these
youngsters are worth every penny. If you have a different
opinion, please be kind enough to explain it."

Her nephew shifted in his chair. His hair had flopped over
his forehead again, but for once he didn't straighten it.
"As you like, Aunt Elizabeth," he said, stiffly. "Go ahead,
if you must."

"I'm so glad you agree, Hugo."

She beamed at Archie, Spud and Lola. "The three of you
have done marvels in the past three days. Especially in such
sweltering conditions. You must be so relieved it's over!"

"Not quite over," said Archie.

He'd been cradling the vase in his arms. As he lowered it on to the table, he let it slip clear of the sack so that it stood there in all its splendour – the most colourful object by far amongst the tea things.

"We found this vase in a sack snagged on a nail at the back of a cupboard," he said. "It must have been there for years and years."

"Good gracious," said Elizabeth.

She bent forward in her chair, jiggling the spectacles on her nose as if to bring the vase into focus. As she turned it this way and that, they could sense memories flooding back. "I haven't seen this for years," she said. "Not since I was a young woman. The vase is Chinese, you know – a memento of a visit long ago when the seventh Lord Hartnip was a Government envoy. Apparently it was a gift from the Chinese Government."

56

"A bit of family history," said Hugo, dryly. "A reminder of the kind of people we were in former days."

The old lady sighed and picked the vase up. Gently, she began to stroke it like Aladdin summoning the genie from his lamp. Her eyes were bright with the wishes she'd love to make. Archie shot a look at Spud and Lola. They both nodded eagerly. "Er ... Elizabeth?" Archie said.

"Yes, my dear?"

"We think we've got some really good news. Lola recognised this vase almost at once. It's just like one Mr Danziger talked about at Art Club. So we looked it up on the internet. A vase that's exactly the same as this was auctioned for £50 million!"

Elizabeth smiled slightly. "Alas, not exactly the same," she said.

"Isn't it?"

"Every detail is correct, of course. But it isn't quite the real thing. The original Emperor's vase was sold long before I was born. For all I know, it may have been the very one that came up at last year's auction. This one is like everything else in the house, I'm sorry to say."

"You mean it's a fake?"

"We prefer to call it a copy, Archie," said Elizabeth with a faraway look in her eyes.

9. FIRE AND WATER

Later, after they'd collected their wages and said goodbye, they saw the funny side of what had happened.

"A fake," Spud spluttered. "All that worrying about what we should do ... and the vase was only a fake!"

"Good job we talked to your mum, Archie," said Lola.

Archie looked up at the windows of his house. "Yeah," he said, "she's not daft, my mum. She won't be home from work yet. Want to come up and wait for her? We can tell her all about it."

"Why not?" Lola grinned. "Even Hugo had a smile on his face when he drove off after tea. Where did he say he was going?"

"To see their bank manager. About organising a loan for the next batch of repairs to the house."

"Good luck to him, Spud. I can't see … "

Lola was cut off by a flash of lightning. Almost instantly, a clap of thunder followed. The noise was so sudden and so deafening that they all ducked as if they'd been struck themselves. There was no blue in the sky now.
From horizon to horizon, a slab of cloud hung over the city like the underside of a giant tombstone.

They were staring south across the river so they couldn't miss the next bolt of lightning. In the longest split-second of their lives it seemed to sizzle out of the blackness and shake the Big House from end to end.

"That was a direct hit!" yelped Spud.

"Will it set the roof on fire?" Lola gasped.

"Maybe it has already. And underneath it is the attic where we've got everything piled up like a line of bonfires."

"Got your mobile, Spud?" Archie snapped.

"Yeah, but it's so old – "

"Try it."

Spud fumbled in his pocket. Twice he managed to misdial the emergency services but the third time he got through.

Archie and Lola listened anxiously, as the operator
went step by step through the emergency procedure.
"They're on their way," Spud said at last,
"coming as fast as they can."

"Yeah," said Lola, "on a Friday in the rush hour."

"With Elizabeth on her own," Spud gulped.

"Let's go back!"

"Not by the road," Archie said. "This way's quicker."

Already he was heading for the Quaggy. They scrambled over its ramshackle fencing and slid down the low, rough-cast slope to the riverbed. The dried mud, junk and shallow puddles were easier to cope with than they'd expected. True, the bank on the far side was steeper and harder to climb, but even that didn't delay them long. Not with a touch of panic spurring them on.

"Made it!" Archie exclaimed.

After this, they ran so fast across the ruined garden that all three of them had a stitch in their sides before they reached the Big House. To their relief, Hugo had left the outside doors on the latch. It was the inside doors they couldn't open. Frantically, they banged at them with clenched fists.

"Elizabeth!" they shouted. "Elizabeth!"

"She can't hear us!" wailed Spud and Lola.

"Leave it to me," said Archie.

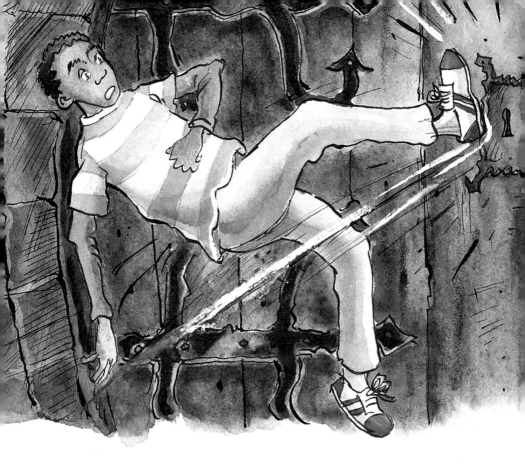

He kicked the iron lock dead centre with the heel of his
heavy-duty trainers. The doors sprang back at once. "We
need to spread out," he said. "She could be anywhere in
the house. Lola, go down to the kitchens. Spud, check all
the other rooms on this floor. I'll try upstairs. If you find her,
yell your head off so that the other two come running."

"Suppose ... suppose we can't find her?" Spud faltered.

"Don't suppose, just do it!"

Lola's footsteps on the stony floor of
the basement and Spud's door-clattering
along the corridor echoed clearly up to
Archie as he climbed the main stairs two
at a time. He barely glanced to right and left.
It was as if he'd known where to look
all along.

Above him was the open trapdoor.

The roof wasn't on fire yet, but Archie knew
it wouldn't be long before the piles
of rubbish were ablaze. "Elizabeth!" he
called again. "Elizabeth!"

"Is that you, Archie?"

Her voice was faint but so close he even heard the catch of relief in her throat. Archie threw his head back and yelled. "Spud! Lola! I've found her, OK! She's up here in the attic!" He scrambled up the narrow steps. She was half-slumped across the lid of the trapdoor.

"Did you come back to save me, my dear?" she smiled.

Archie heaved himself deftly through the gap and into the attic. "What are you doing up here?" he demanded.

"I came to see the finished job, Archie. It seemed so rude that Hugo didn't bother after grumbling about your wages. Then, as I was about to climb down again, there was a tremendous bang. I was so startled my glasses fell off. I didn't dare to make a move without them."

"They're here," said Archie, "by your elbow."

"So they are!"

"Archie?" Spud called from below.

"Elizabeth?" added Lola.

"She's a bit shocked, I think," said Archie. "We need to keep her steady. And get out of here as fast as we can."

Taking turns, they half-propped, half-carried Elizabeth
out of the Big House. For her, the quick route across the
Quaggy was out of the question, so they made for the road
bridge instead. With almost every step, she gazed back at
the way they'd come. There was a second bolt of lightning.
Soon mad turrets of flame licked and spat along the roof.
The fire had the house in its grip now. The windows on the
floors below looked ready to bulge and shatter from the
growing furnace inside.

"It's beginning to rain," Spud said. "Too late to save the house, though."

The rain was soon so fast and heavy that it drove them under the road bridge for shelter. Elizabeth peered intently across the superstore's car park and across her own ravaged garden, both awash with the downpour. She spoke softly to herself.

"Sorry?" Lola blinked. "What did you say?"

"Good riddance."

"What?"

"To that old monster, my dears."

"The Big House, you mean?" said Spud. "But it's your home and it's burning down!"

"I know," Elizabeth murmured, "it's such a relief."

"You mean you don't mind?"

"Of course I mind, Spud. How could I not mind? As a Hartnip, I've always been duty-bound to protect the family house. But there's never been a single day of my life – not one – when I didn't feel the place was crushing me. Oh, I didn't dare admit such a thing. Not even to myself. And especially not to Hugo. Now, though, one flash of lightning has set me free. Can't you see what a release that is?"

"Well," said Lola, faintly, "at least you've got the vase ..."

"The vase?"

"It's here under my arm. I picked it up from the terrace as we passed. I know it's only a fake, but I thought you'd want to keep it."

In the odd half-light under the bridge, Elizabeth smiled wryly. "Bless you, my dear," she said, "but I've always hated that vase as well. For me, it stood for all the family failings I've had to put up with over the years. That's why I stuffed it in the cupboard ages ago."

"It was you who hid it?" Archie exclaimed.

"And then forgot it, yes."

Elizabeth laughed. By the time they heard the sirens from the first of the fire engines, Archie, Spud and Lola were laughing, too. But none of them laughed as loudly, or as long, as Lady Hartnip.

10. DISNEYLAND

Elizabeth's letter was written on smooth, creamy paper in a neat, old-fashioned hand:

My dear Archie, Spud and Lola,

Please forgive my delay in getting in touch. Everything has happened so quickly it's been hard for me to keep up.

As I expect you can see for yourselves, what's left of the Big House is being demolished and the land around it redeveloped. I should be sorry about this, I suppose. And maybe I am, deep down. My main feeling, though, after all those years of struggle to keep the place going, is still one of relief. According to my clever nephew, I can expect enough money from the deal he's done to keep me in comfort for the rest of my life.

Of course, my life might have ended already if the three of you hadn't come to my rescue. What heroes you were! I've been wracking my brains ever since to find a way of saying thank you. Then I thought of the vase you found (twice over). As a copy, it's worth nothing like the original, but apparently it still has considerable value as an oddity – an amount that really surprised me when I asked an expert. So I'm enclosing a cheque, made payable to Archie's lovely mum, to be split between you. It's called a Finder's Fee, I believe. Please spend it on some trip or treat that you'll never forget.

With all my love and gratitude,
Elizabeth Hartnip

Archie, Spud and Lola read the letter over and over again –
so often, in fact, that they pretty much learnt it by heart.

They agreed at once what to do with the money.

Times change ... and a sensible person – Hartnip or otherwise – changes with them.

The Bi

trouble o

This house was built for our family more than 400 years ago. We've lived here ever since – Hartnip after Hartnip.

Will he really let her restore the Big House to its former glory? He'll see it as wasting millions of pounds on a project that's completely pointless.

It's their house, their vase and their decision, OK? Nobody can make it for them.

House – treasure?

There's never been a single day of my life – not one – when I didn't feel the place was crushing me. Now, though, one flash of lightning has set me free.

Ideas for reading

Written by Clare Dowdall, PhD
Lecturer and Primary Literacy Consultant

Learning objectives: understand underlying themes, causes and points of view; understand how writers use different structures to create coherence and impact; recognise rhetorical devices used to argue, persuade, mislead and sway the reader; sustain engagement with longer texts; improvise using a range of drama strategies and conventions to explore themes; select words and language drawing on their knowledge of literary features and formal and informal writing

Curriculum links: Citizenship: Choices; Art: Visiting a museum, gallery or site

Interest words: mirage, heritage, tycoon, memento, auctioned, oddity

Resources: pen, paper, whiteboard

Getting started

This book can be read over two or more reading sessions.

- Ask children to consider the image on the front cover and discuss the house. What do they expect it to look like inside? Have they ever visited a house like this or seen pictures of similar existing houses?

- Discuss what the Quaggy might be and ask children to justify their ideas. If needed, explain that it is the name of a river.

- Read the blurb and ask children to predict what may be special about the house, and what might happen in the story.

Reading and responding

- Ask children to read to p9 silently. On p8, focus on the sentence, "He seemed to be weighing his words as he spoke." Discuss the meaning of the words and the effect they have on the reader.

- Ask children to read to p45 and suggest different options the characters will be considering now they think the vase is worth a lot of money. What would the children do themselves if they were in a similar situation?

- Ask children to read to the end of the story independently, noting the high points of tension that the author creates.